HOW TO DRAW SONIC

STEP-BY-STEP

#BEST SELLER BOOK

SONIC

THIS BOOK BELONGS TO

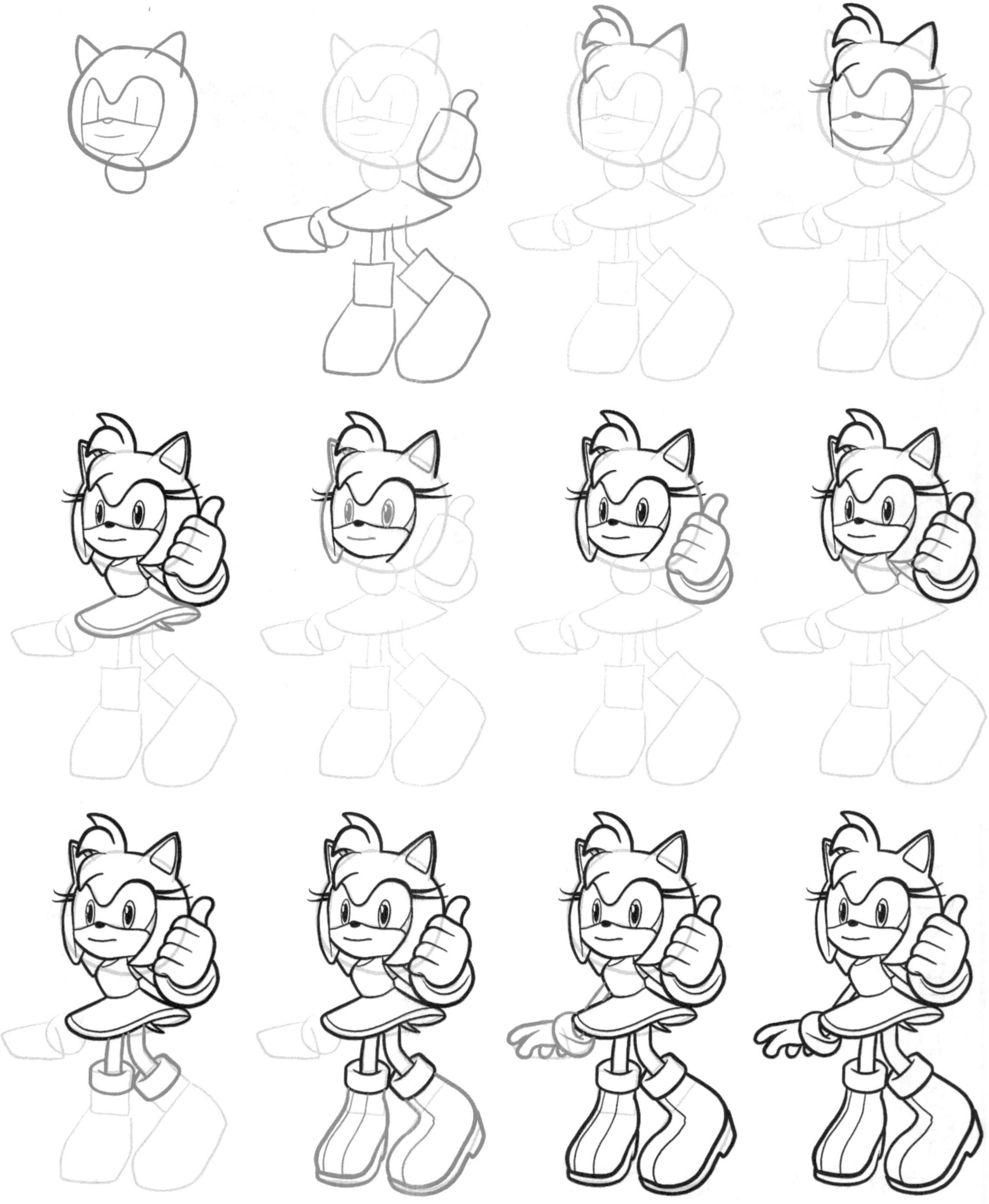

DRAWING TUTORIAL

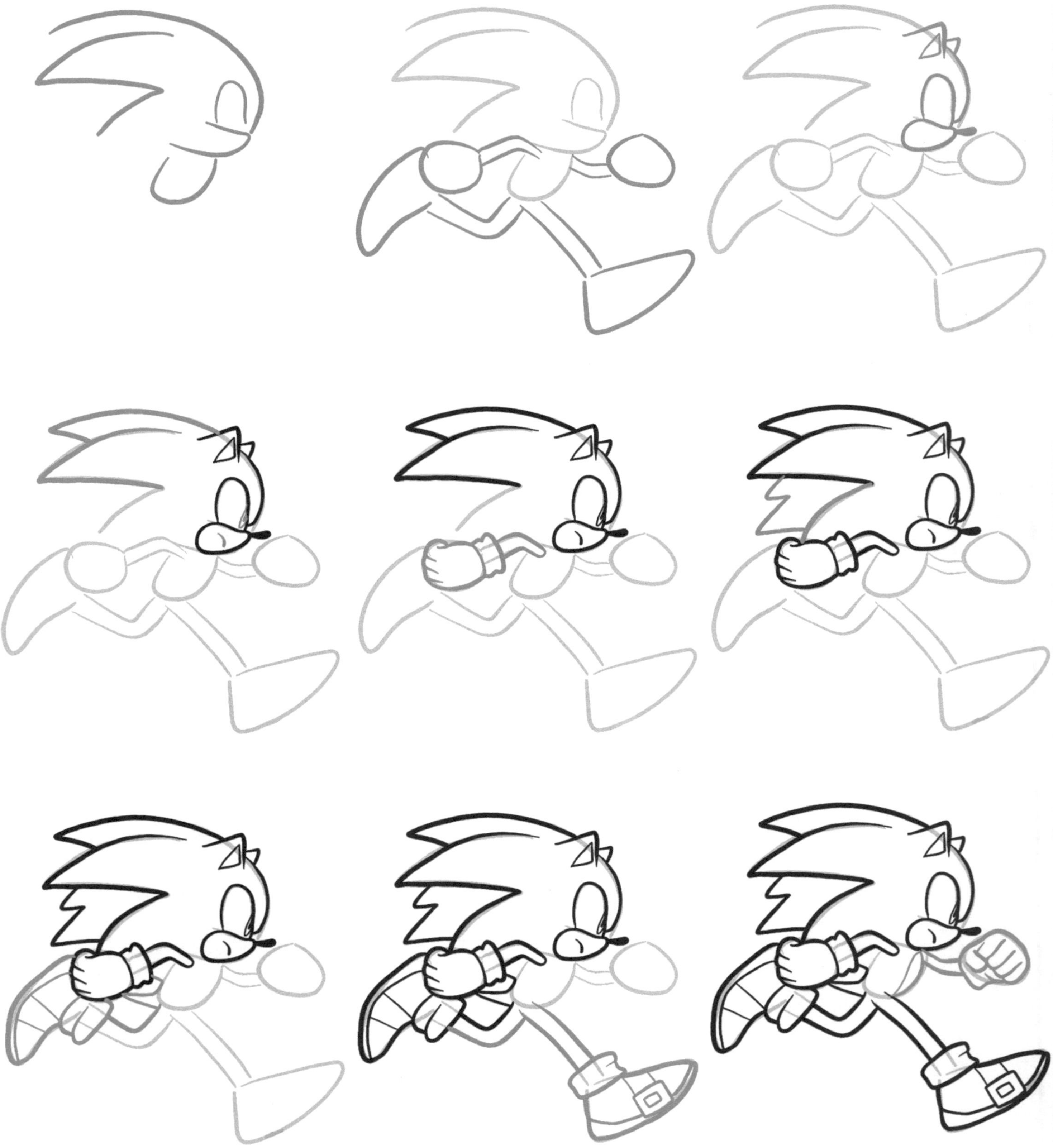

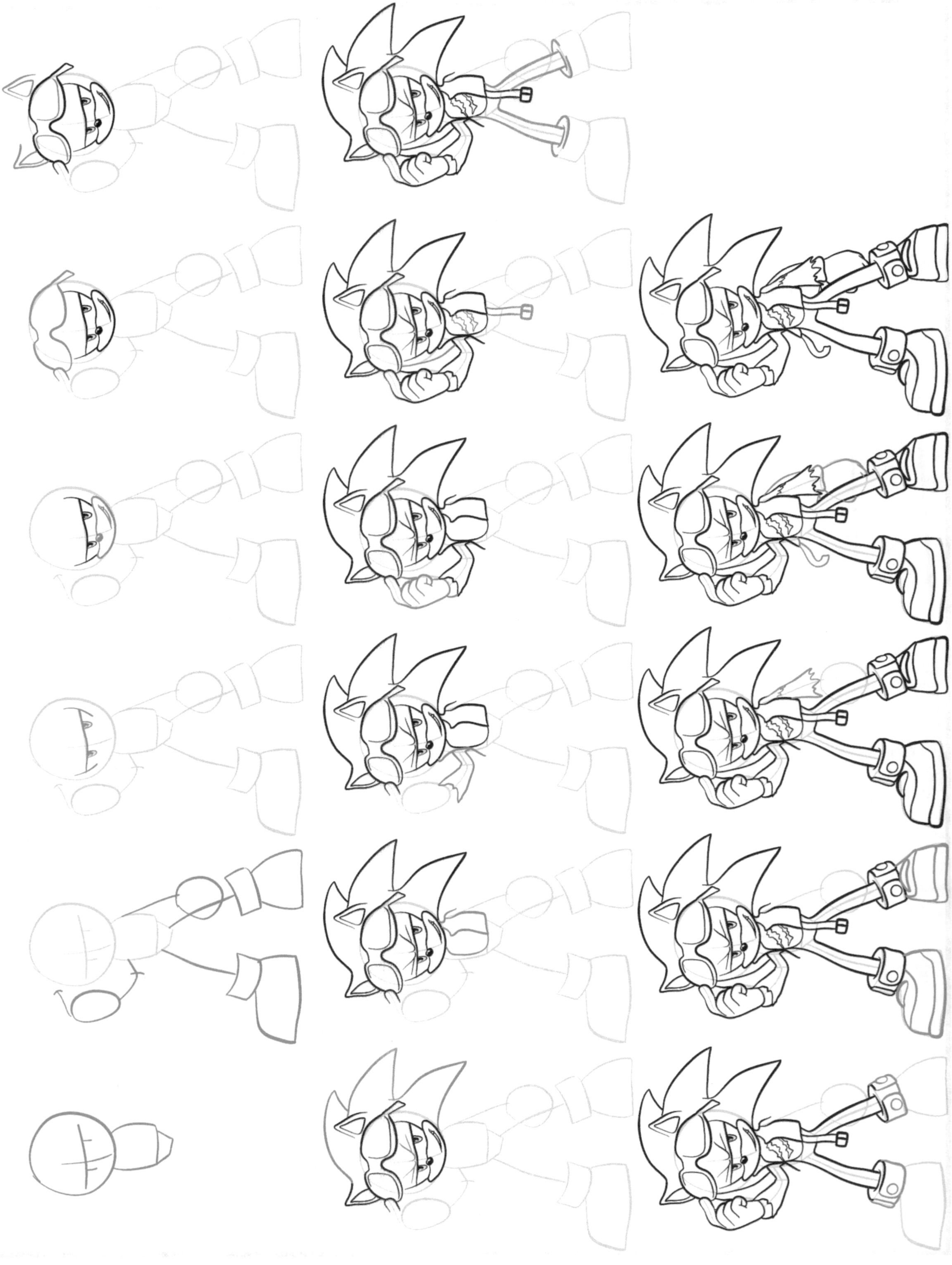

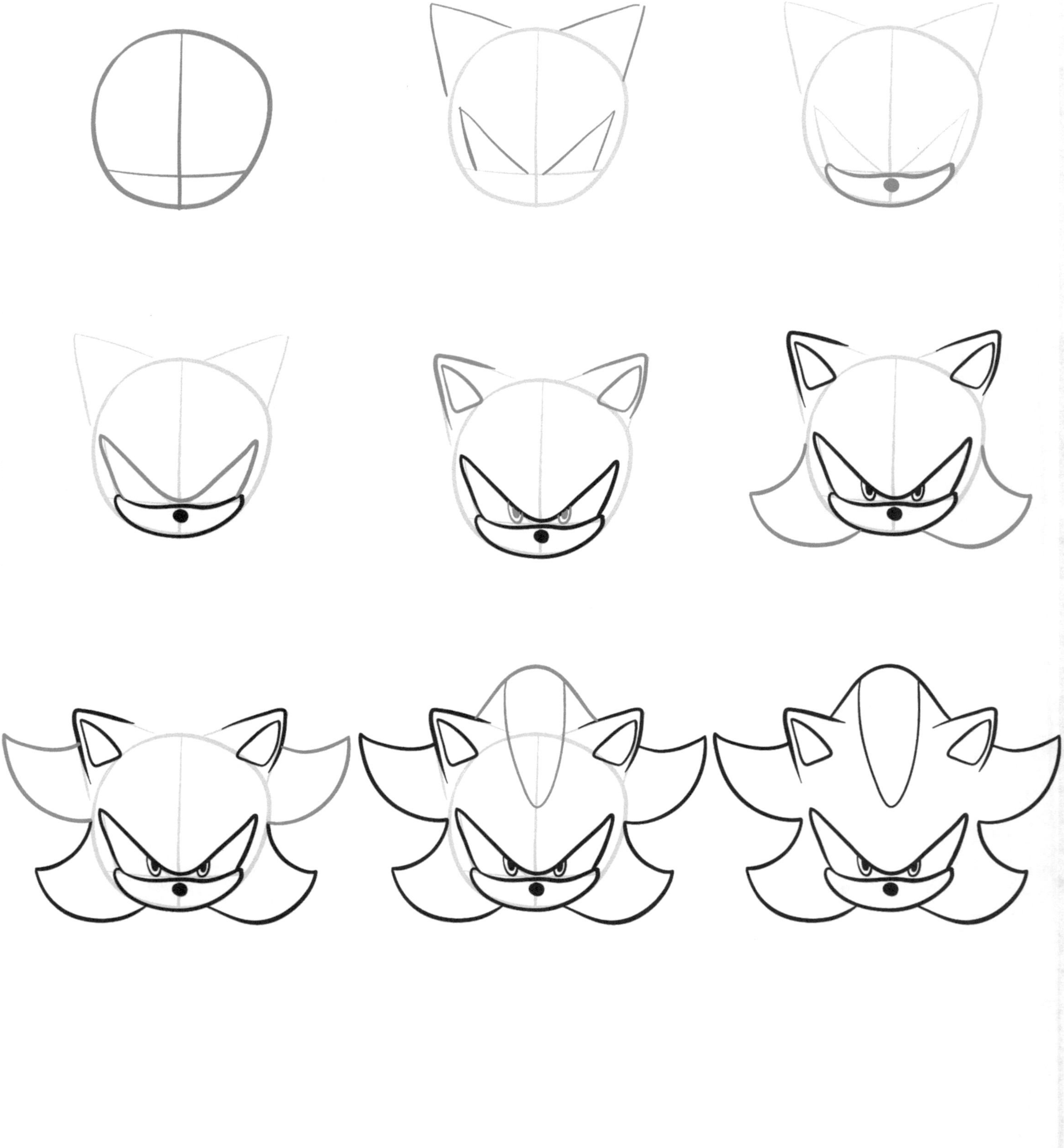

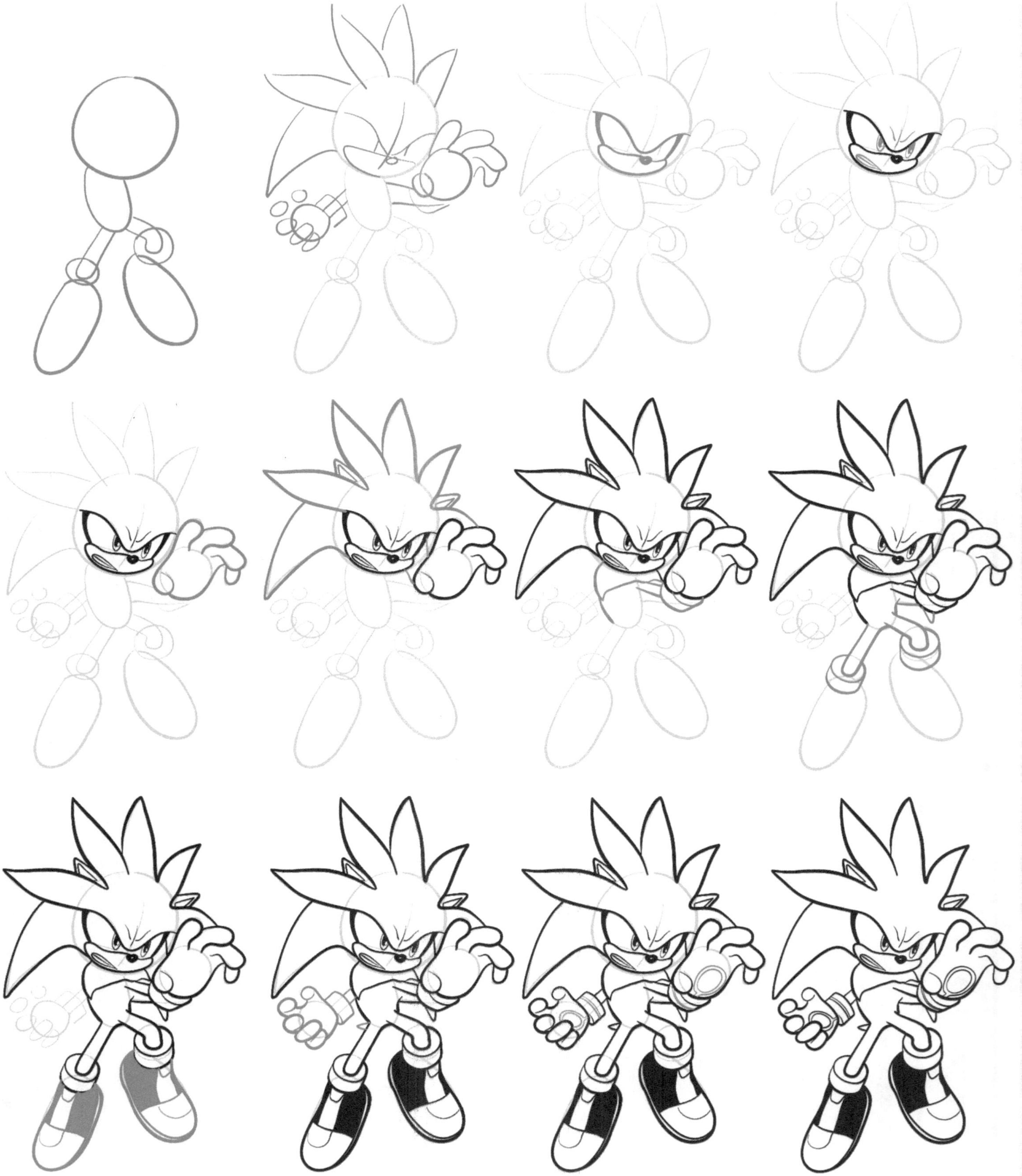

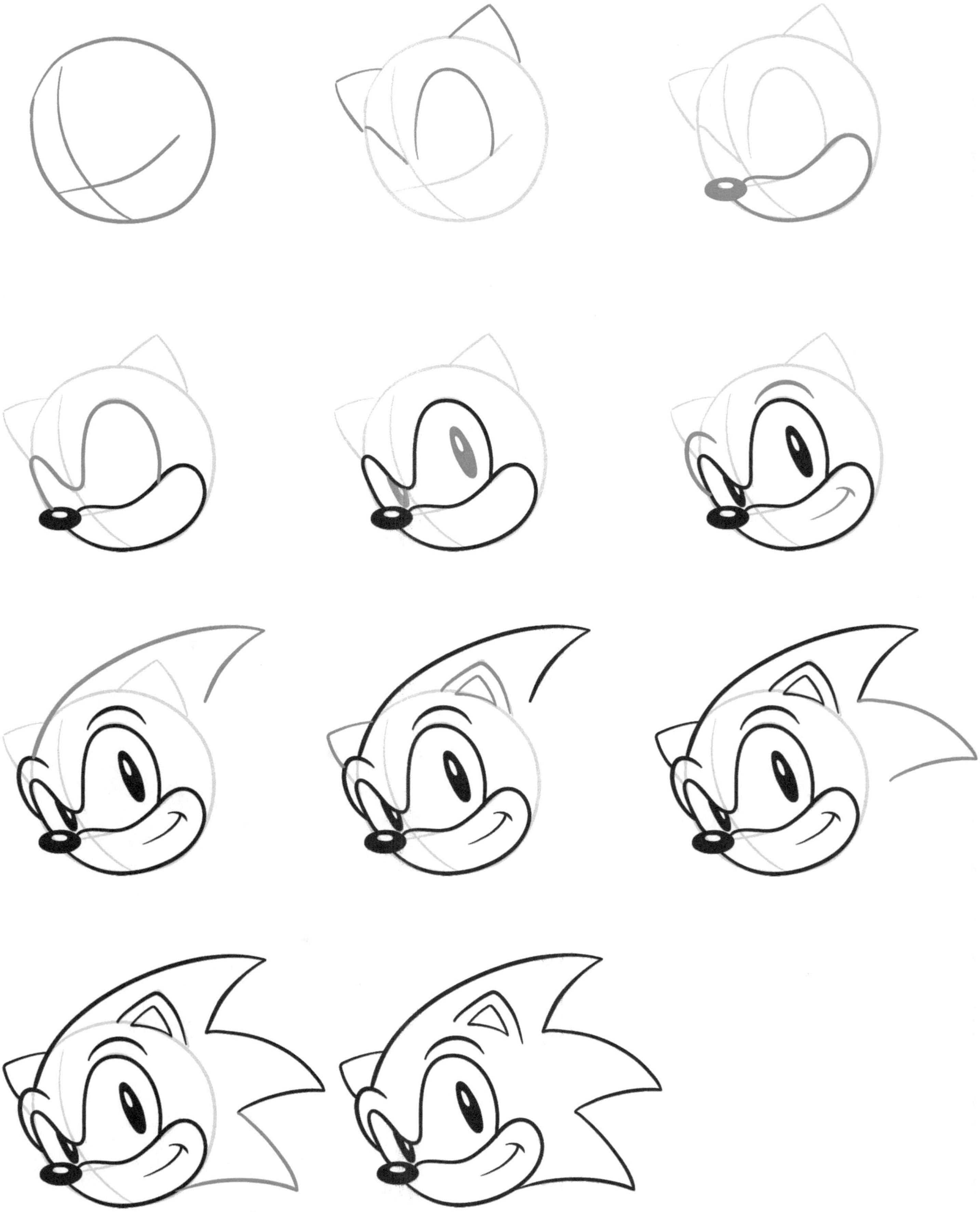

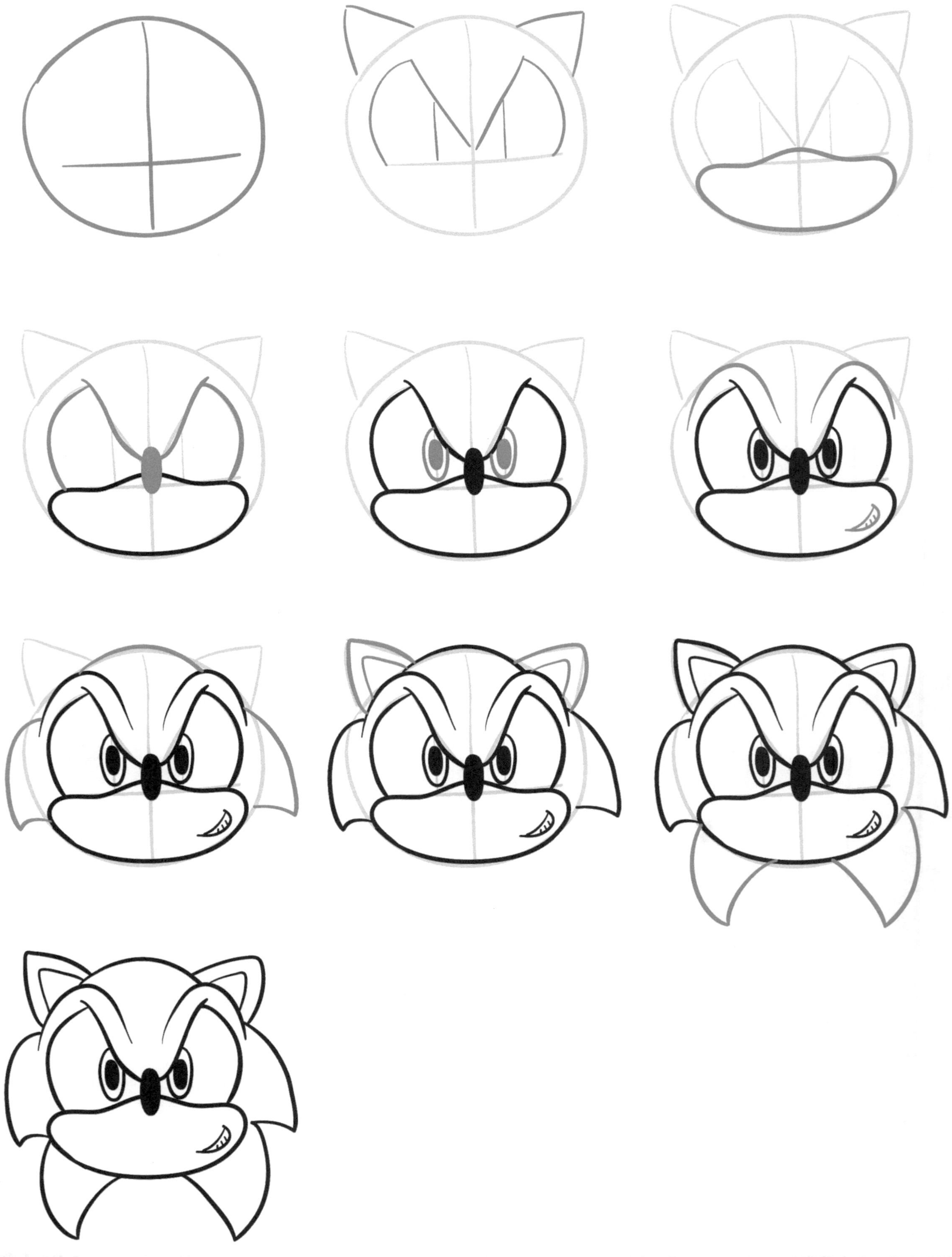

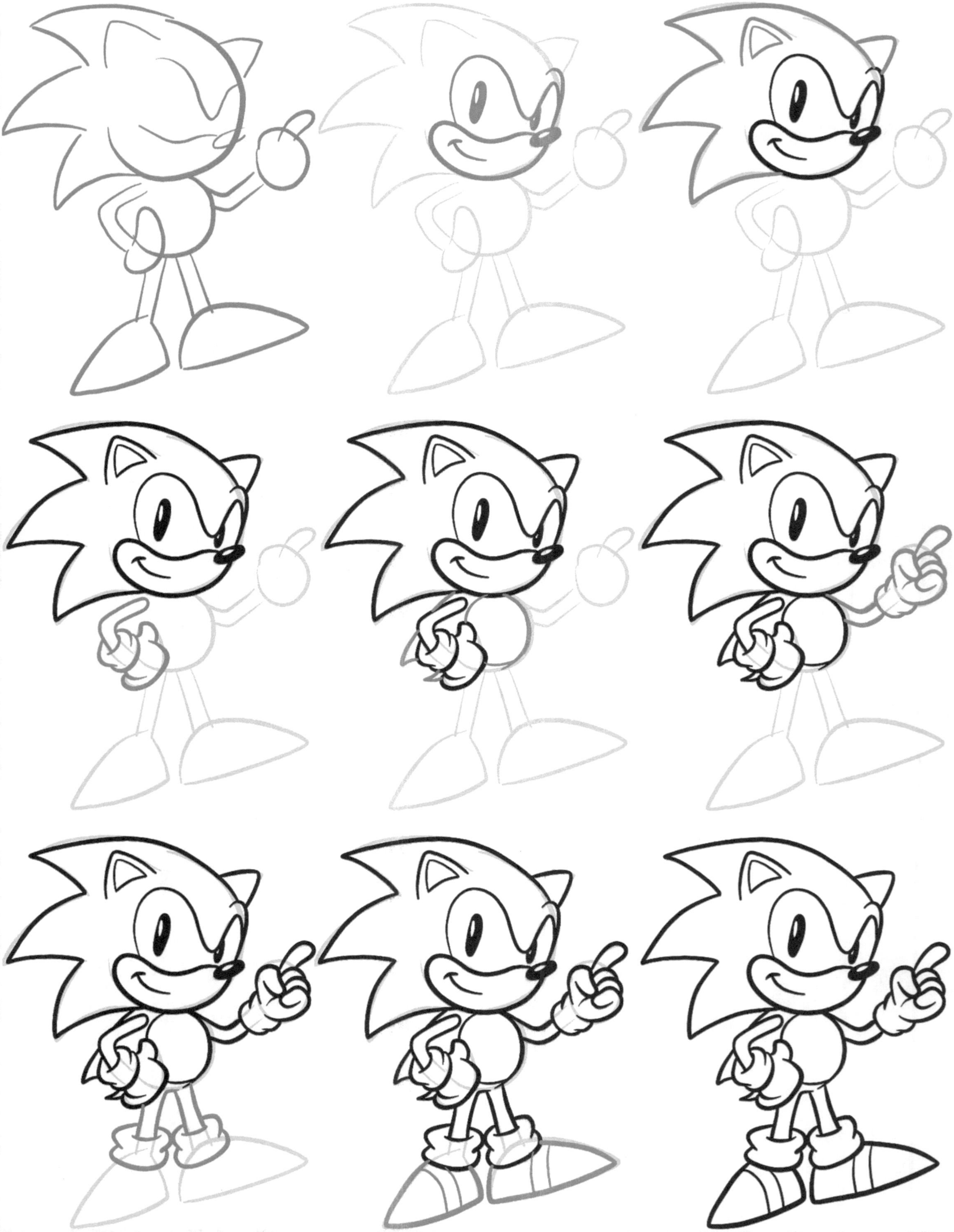

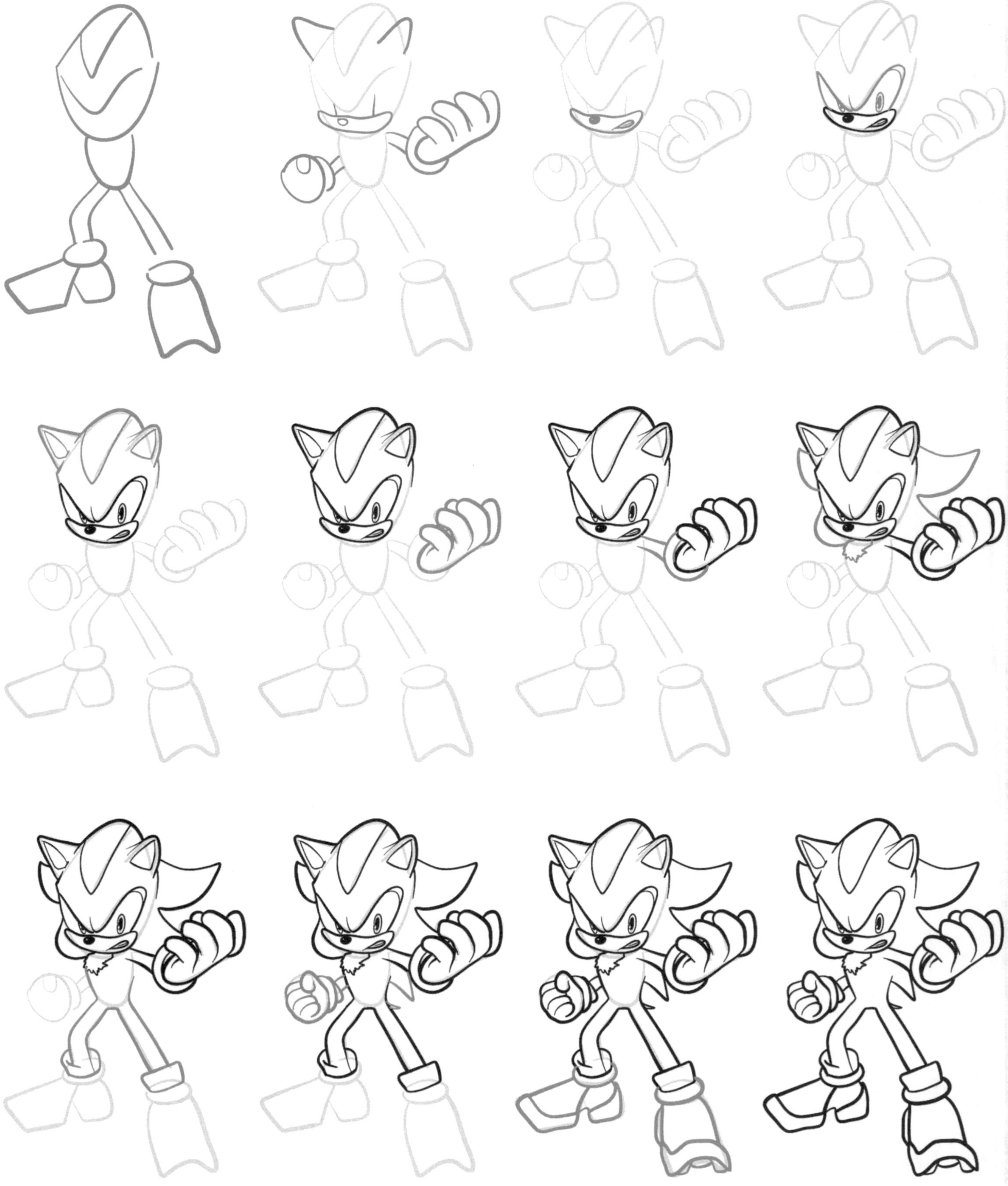

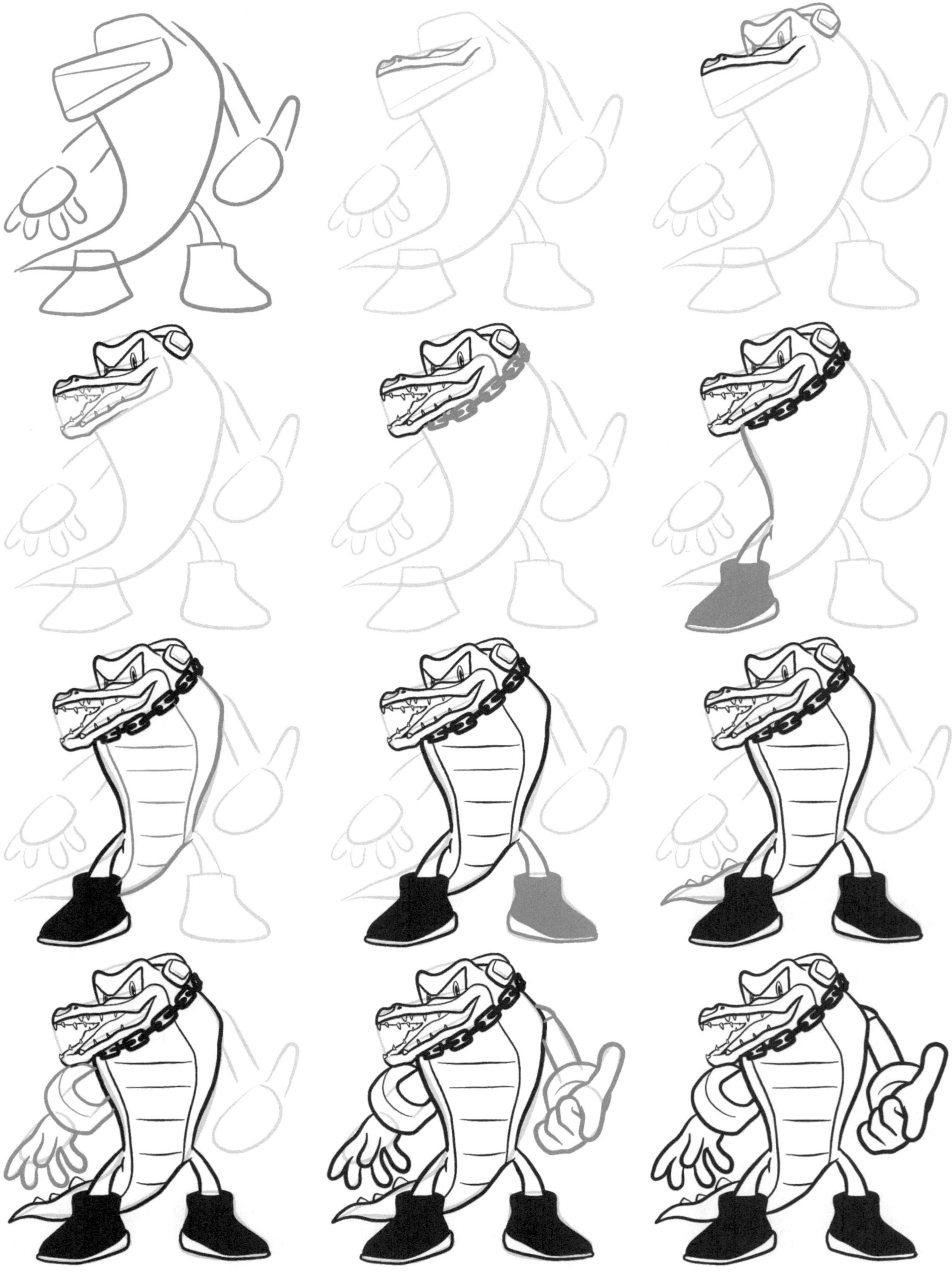

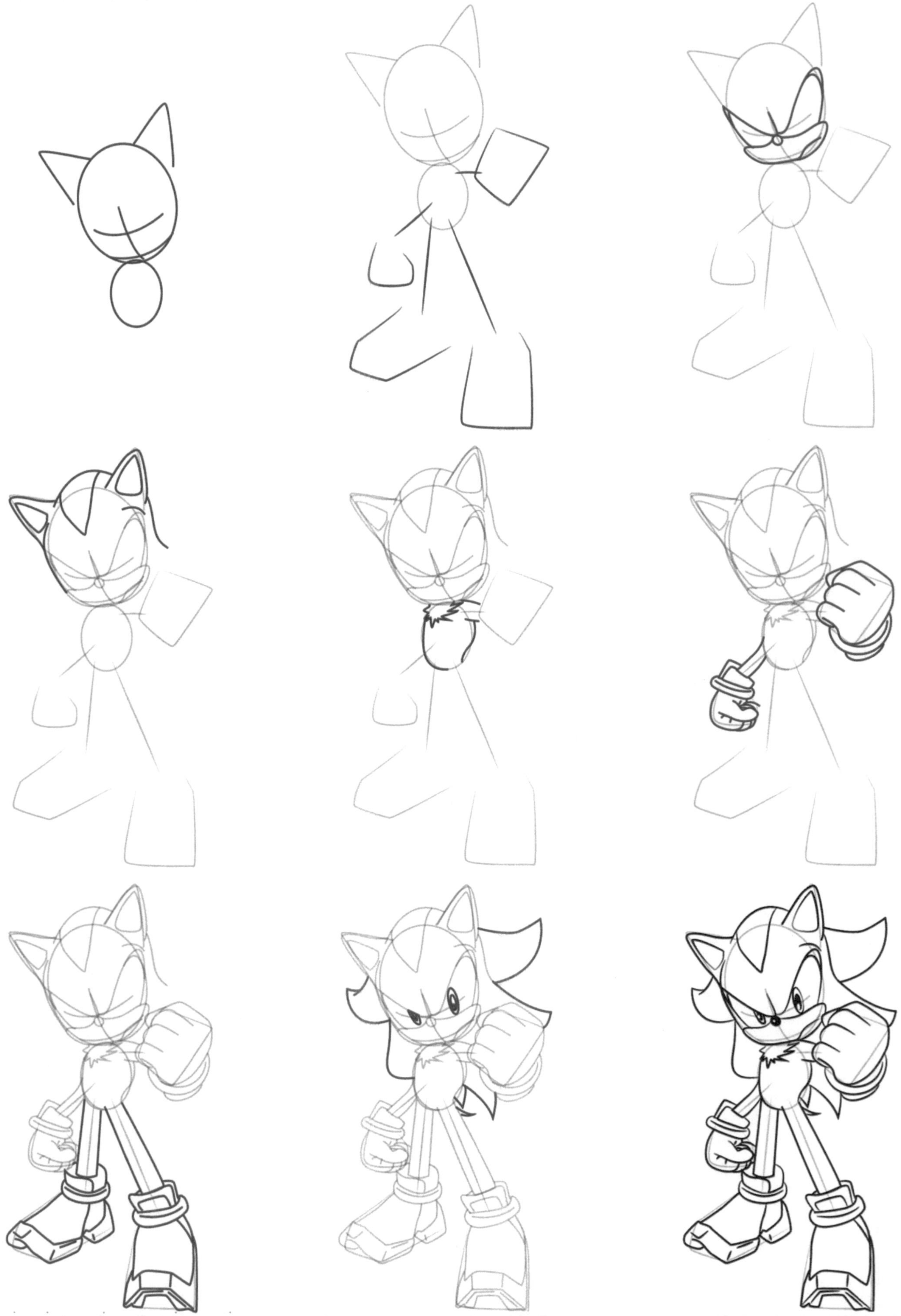

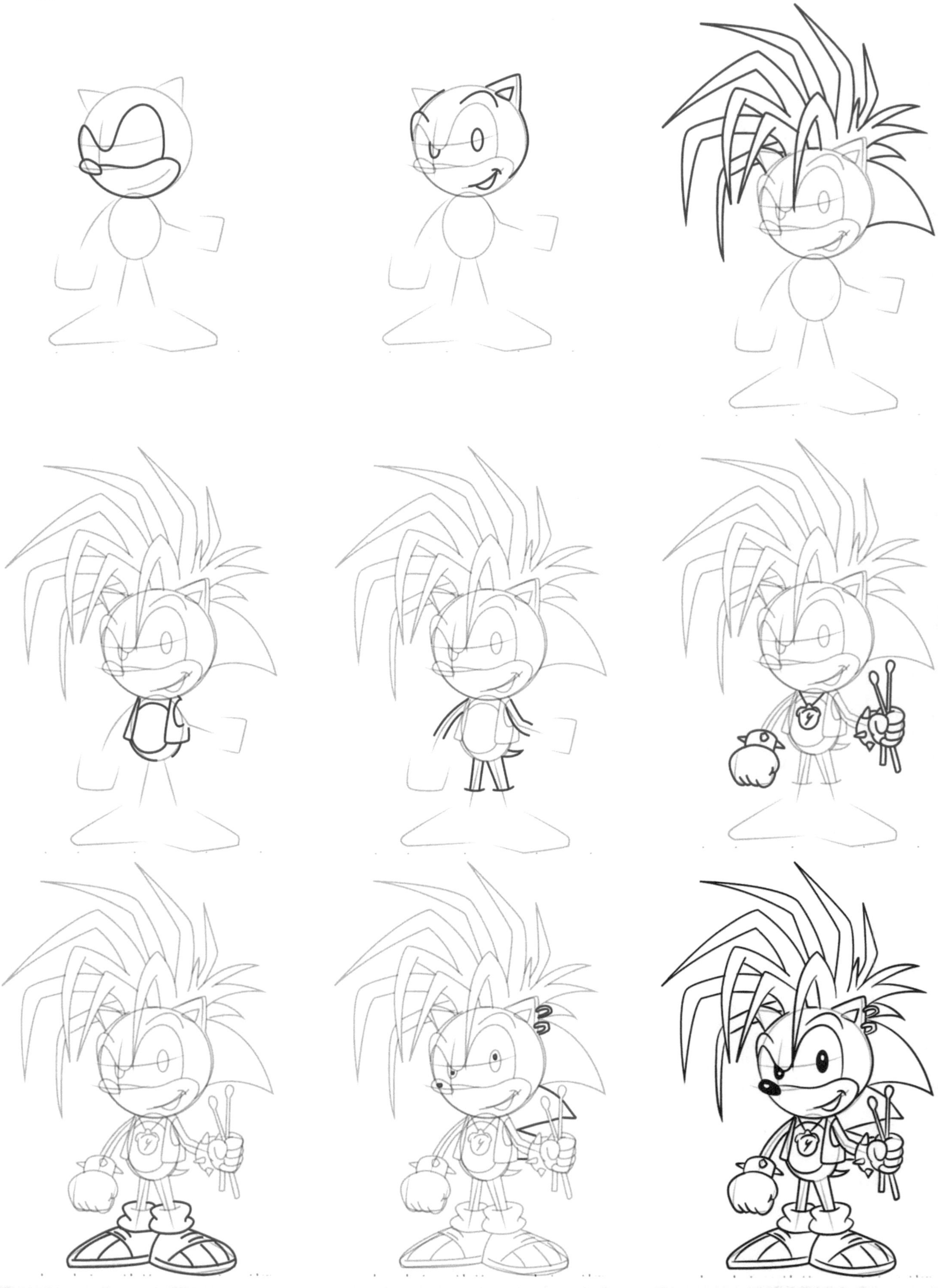

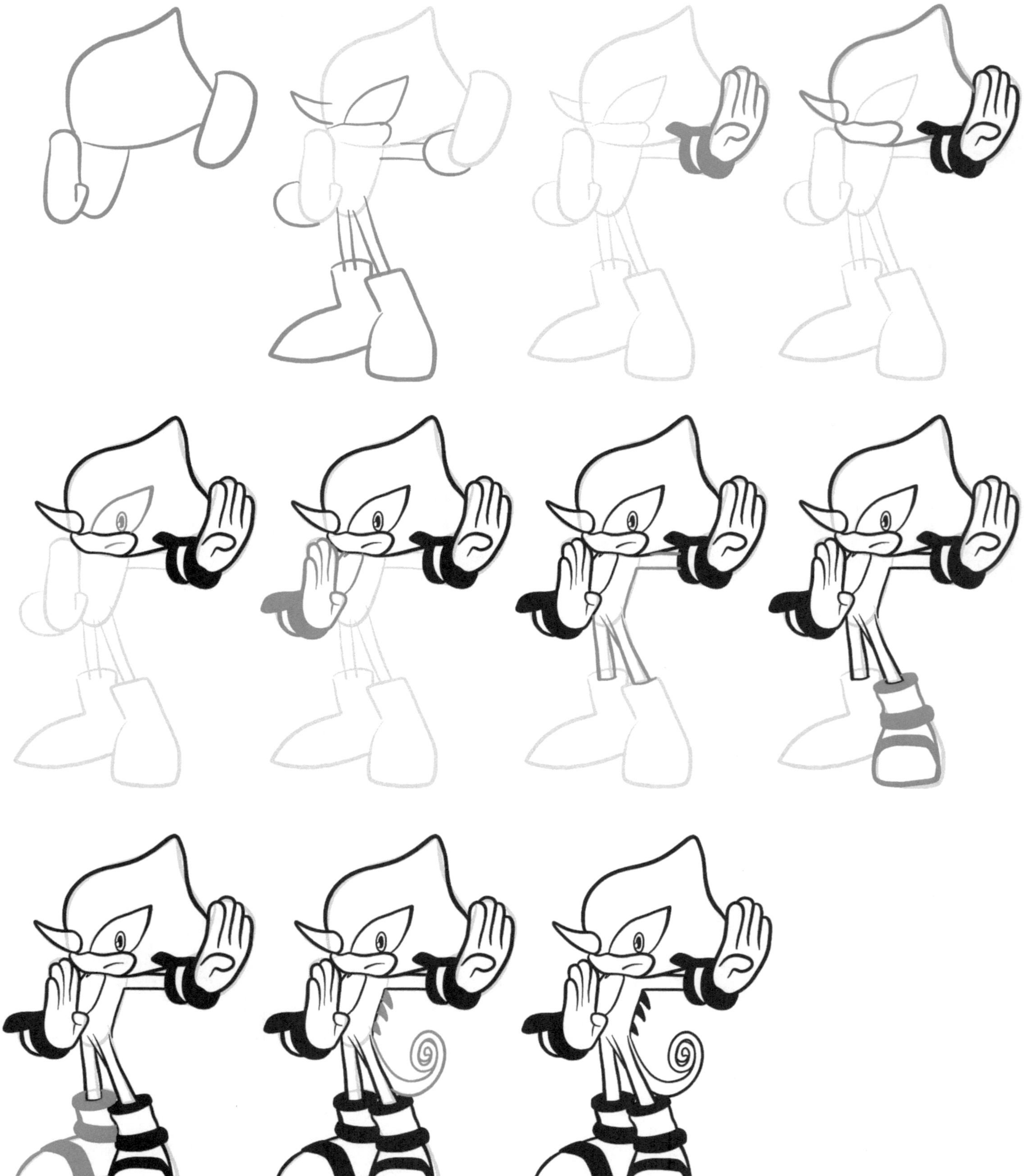

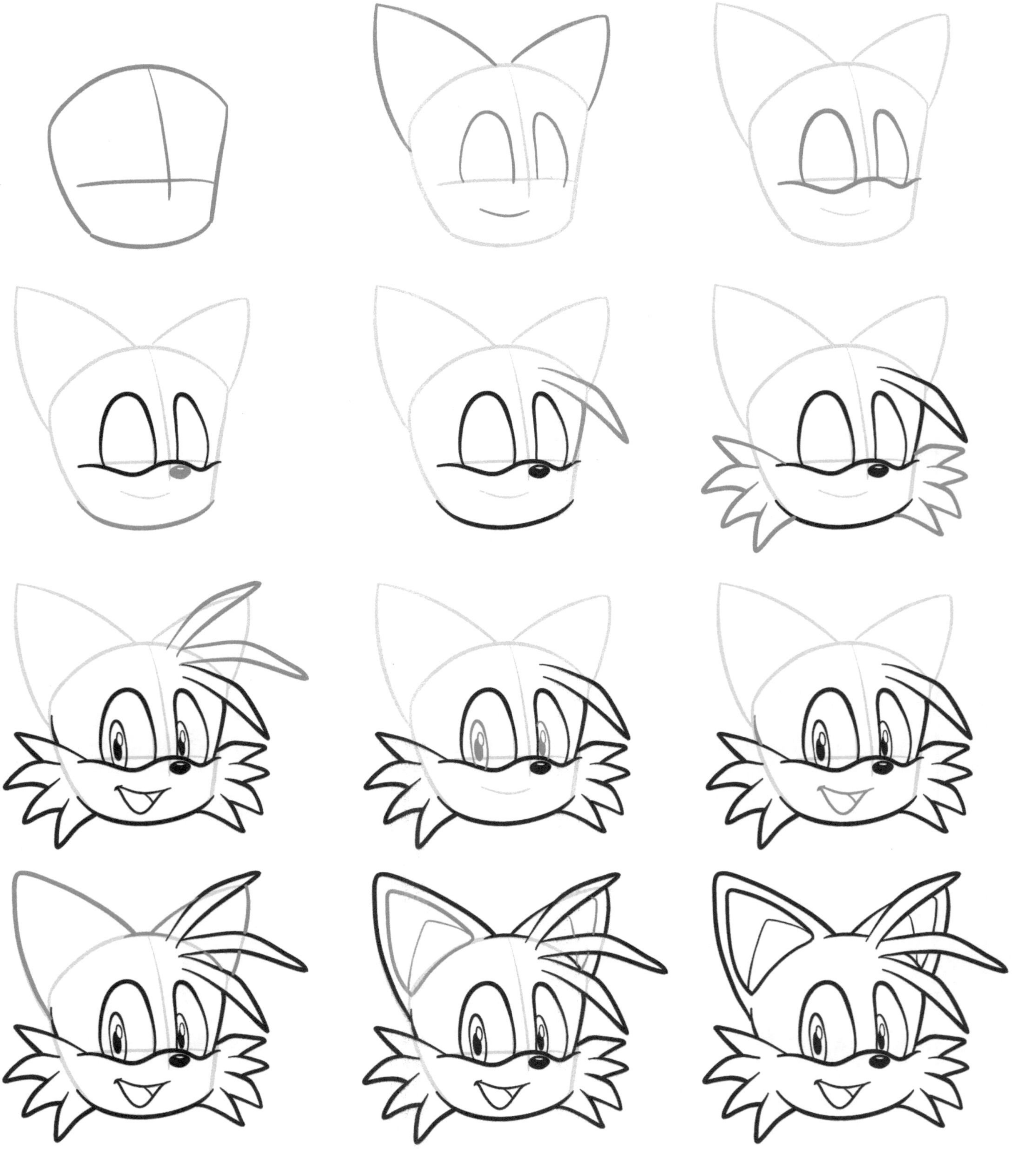

Made in United States
Troutdale, OR
05/01/2024

19593474R00038